It's the witching hour of night and two shadowy figures are stealing ac... People's P... rk. One ... bushma... aw and t... minute... ter, the sk... are in ... iver.

Nat... ly there's blue murder and Mrs O'Lea... now Councillor O'Leary, in spite of all ... hard work tearing down and defac... her election posters and shouting insult... rough keyholes) springs into actio... andbag at the ready.

Riv... de Boys v the GAA is on!

In b... veen skirmishes, Chippy has a great i... ea, Brains O'Mahony has another, and Mad Victor and Mad Henry see a bit of the world.

Jimmy has something else on his mind – who, in the absence of his masterpiece, *Forlorn Love,* will win the Book-of-the-Year Award!

Peter Regan

RIVERSIDE

The Croke Park Conspiracy

Illustrated by Terry Myler

THE CHILDREN'S PRESS

For

Laura and Grandad Eamonn

First published 1997 by
The Children's Press
an imprint of Anvil Books
45 Palmerston Road, Dublin 6

4 6 5 3

ISBN 1 901737 04 7

Typeset by Computertype Limited
Printed by Colour Books Limited

Contents

1 Mrs O'Leary's Bombshell

Mrs O'Leary is a woman I don't get on with. None of my pals, Chippy O'Brien, Mad Victor or Flintstone McKay get on with her either. If you called her an oul' crow you wouldn't be telling lies.

We had local Council elections here in Bray the other week. Mrs O'Leary stood and won. Me and my pals were disappointed she got elected. We were hoping she'd get nowhere, except dumped in the sea for her trouble. We did everything possible to stop her being elected. At least, I did.

And who am I? Just call me Jimmy – Jimmy Quinn. I'm a real gentleman, so my ma says. She should know; she's been around long enough.

Soon as Mrs O'Leary won her seat on the local Council she began to throw her weight about.

The People's Park, where Riverside Boys, my club team, play all their football, is a council pitch, and as soon as Mrs O'Leary came into office she began to eye it for one of the local GAA clubs.

GAA stands for Gaelic Athletic Association, in case you're not into sport. They're into hurling, and a class of football they call Gaelic. Camogie too. That's for girls.

Mr Glynn and Harry Hennessy became very wary of Mrs O'Leary once they heard about that.

Mr Glynn is real nice. He works as a salesman for a sweets company and he is always giving us chocolate and sweets. Mad Victor loves going in his car because there are always sweets in it, sometimes in boxes, other times stuck in gaps between the seats. Lately Mr Glynn started carrying bubble gum in the car and Mad Victor was nuts on it. He could blow bubbles the size of his head with the stuff.

We started having competitions with the gum, but Mad Victor always won. One time he blew a bubble so big that it flopped all the way down to his knees. We went to get a camera to take a photograph, but by the time we got back it had burst and was stuck to his jumper and trousers like bits of scraped, dried paint.

Harry Hennessy isn't like Mr Glynn. He hasn't any sweets, but even if he had, he'd never give us any like Mr Glynn does. But we like him anyway. He's big and fat. So fat that if he fell down we reckon he wouldn't be able to get back up again.

We have a mountain in Bray. Well, a few mountains. Some of us, when we look at Harry, him being so big and that, we think of him as one of the mountains – the Sugarloaf. But we never call him that. We like him too much.

Harry used to be a referee. But he gave all that up because he was getting fatter and fatter all the time. He was afraid he'd die of a heart attack. Harry is Mr Glynn's right-hand man. He helps Mr Glynn with the team. Sometimes he comes to the matches drunk, but not very often. We all know where he goes after matches, though. He goes to the pub. And we all know what happens after that. He goes home drunk.

The first we knew of Mrs O'Leary wanting to get her hands on the People's Park was when we overheard Harry Hennessy and Mr Glynn talking about it.

'Mrs O'Leary's after the Park?'

'She's tryin' to get Eddie Marsden in on it.'

'Is that the lad that runs the GAA club?'

'Sure. Him and his wife Margo.'

'She says they only want it for the summer. But once they get in they'll take over.'

'The nerve! Haven't they plenty of other pitches without wantin' the Park?'

'They say the Park would be handy – it's just down the road for the kids – and as we don't use it during the summer it wouldn't be puttin' anyone out.'

'Except us, when the soccer season starts. Not likely, not damned likely. We'll fight tooth and nail. They'll not get in on the Park.'

But they did. Eddie Marsden and Margo, with the help of Mrs O'Leary, took over the Park. They slapped their Gaelic posts right on our soccer pitch. When we went down to the Park one day the posts were up, like skinny sky-

scrapers, lording it over every blade of grass in sight.

We rang Mr Glynn straight away.

'What'll we do, Mr Glynn? They've put the Gaelic posts right on our pitch?'

'What! Are you sure?'

'We're jus' after comin' from there. They're up all right.'

'We'll call a meetin' for tomorrow night.'

'Where, Mr Glynn?'

'Where, what?'

'Where's the meetin'?'

'Around at my house. Seven-thirty.'

At the meeting Mrs O'Leary, Eddie Marsden, Margo and the goal-posts were the main subject of discussion. We were all there, the whole team. We gave Eddie Marsden a right going-over.

'He's in the IRA, ye know.'

'Course I know. Everyone knows. That's why his nickname is 3-0-3.'

'Why 3-0-3?'

'Cause 3-0-3 is a rifle they used to use in the First World War. 3-0-3 Marsden is what we call him.'

'Don't know what he's doin' mixed up with the IRA. Cause Marsden is an English name. Ever hear of Jerry an' the Pacemakers?'

'Naw.'

'Well, they're from England. They sang that song *Ferry Cross the Mersey*. An' their lead singer, Jerry Marsden, sang Liverpool's song *You'll Never Walk Alone*. He was the first to ever sing it.'

'What's that got to do with Eddie Marsden?'

'Well, it proves that Marsden is an English name.'

'Suppose so.'

Unknown to Mr Glynn and Harry Hennessy, later that night me and Chippy O'Brien wrote a few words on the lower gable-end wall of Eddie Marsden's GAA club-house:

Edy and Margo Marsdin:
Bank robers and landgrabers.
Mrs O'Leary is the saim to.

The same night, Harry Hennessy and Mad Victor met up when the pubs closed, and went to the Park. Harry had a bushman saw, and Mad Victor showed him the way in case the Guinness had blurred his vision. It only took a few minutes to saw down the goal-posts. Luckily, they fell the right way and nobody was hurt. They carried them over to the river and threw them in. All that was left the next morning were the stumps, about the height of Mad Victor's waist.

There was blue murder over it all. Eddie Marsden went ape, and Mrs O'Leary was stark raving mad. She had it put in the local paper:

'Vandals wreck goal-posts!' it screamed

Vandals?

Heroes more likely.

New goal-posts went up. They were sawn down.

It ended up that there was more sawdust than grass in the Park.

Thing that beats me though – we were never caught!

2 Chippy's Brainwave

I like to write. I think I'm quite good at it.

I have my own room at home for writing in. It's only a box-room, but I let on it's some kind of special place known only to myself. When I'm in that room I write a lot.

Just a few weeks ago I finished writing a short book for a story competition in Dublin. At first I was writing a football story, *Soccer King*. But Chippy O'Brien felt there was no way a soccer story would win a book competition. So he gave me all these new ideas for another book – *Forlorn Love.*

I had Chippy to thank for making sure I was getting on with the job. He was good at that, driving me on, telling me to keep up the good work. He didn't half ask plenty of questions about *Soccer King,* though. Asking me what it was about, what kind of characters were in it, and how it ended.

Still, I didn't mind, because he gave me more

than enough help with *Forlorn Love.* Only for him I probably wouldn't have been able to write it in the first place. Like I've just said, most of the ideas were his anyway. They sounded a bit daft at first, but when I got it all down on paper the story came across pretty well. At least, I thought it did.

With the story completed I was all set for the book competition. But something went wrong with *Forlorn Love.* It went missing. However, I'm still interested in finding out who won. The winner is to be announced at a big 'do' in Dublin later on. I'll be there, just to see what I missed out on. But I won't tell any of the lads. They'd only make a show of me, especially Mad Victor.

I wouldn't mind if Chippy went, but I'm not going to tell him – just in case. He said *Forlorn Love* was great. He called it a blockbuster. I liked that.

Chippy's smart, maybe too smart. His eyes light up once money is mentioned. He's great for thinking up ways to make money. Like the other day, he said we should go into business together.

'Business?'

'We'll get a second-hand wheelbarrow an' sell fruit-'n'-veg.'

'Think we'd do well?'

'Course we will, especially with new potatoes. There's a great profit in new potatoes. We could try some fish as well. Fish is a great money-maker on Fridays.'

'You sure?'

'Course I'm sure.'

Straight away I believed Chippy. He's great at selling things. Until lately he was selling fresh eggs around the houses; that's until it all came to an end. The customers would still remember him, though. There was nothing surer, me and Chippy would make plenty of money. Maybe we'd even get to open a bank-account.

There was plenty to look forward to: crossing swords with Mrs O'Leary and Eddie Marsden, making plenty of money selling fruit-'n'-veg, and going to the 'do' where the winner of the book competition would be announced.

I was that excited, I couldn't wait for it all to happen.

Mr Glynn and Harry Hennessy were called into the Council offices to try and settle the row over the Gaelic posts on our football pitch.

The other half of the row, Eddie Marsden and his wife Margo, were called in too. Mrs O'Leary also showed up. She said she was a 'neutral observer' whatever that was supposed to mean. But she was telling lies. She certainly wasn't on our side, as one of her young lads was going with Eddie Marsden's daughter. Mr Glynn and Harry Hennessy didn't know this, but I did. Mad Victor told me. He saw the two of them in a field, kissing.

The Council official tried to make Mr Glynn, Harry Hennessy and Eddie Marsden come to an agreement over the goal-posts.

'We all know who's sawing down the goal-posts.'

'No, we don't!' roared Harry Hennessy. 'You think it's us, don't you?'

The official kind of muttered. Then he mumbled, 'The goal-posts are only for the summer.'

'For the summer?'

'It's only to allow the GAA club time to have their pitches resodded.'

'That's what *you* think They'll move in permanent. That's the way they work. They'll be on top of us, an' take the whole place over.'

'Mr Marsden's prepared to say that it will only be for the summer. In writing. He's also going to make a set of portable goal-posts that can be placed in front of the GAA posts whenever you feel a need to use the pitch during the summer. What's wrong with that?'

'Doesn't mean the goal-posts won't be cut down.'

'But it will help.'

'What's that supposed to mean?'

'Nothing, except once it's in writing that it's only for the summer and you have access to portable goal-posts, there's nothing to fight about.'

There was a picture on the Council office wall. 'That's Saint Patrick, isn't it?' fumed Harry Hennessy.

'Yes, it's the man himself.'

'Well, some of your crowd stoned him when he first landed in Ireland all them years ago.'

'What do you mean?'

'I mean what I said. Your kind wouldn't let the man near the place. They stoned him, an' you've been stonin' people ever since.'

'That's not a nice comment, Mr Hennessy. We try to do our best for everyone.'

'Try! You'd want to try harder. We don't want that lot near our football pitch.'

But there was nothing Harry Hennessy nor Mr Glynn could do about it. We didn't own the pitch. The man behind the desk did. The man over whom Saint Patrick loomed, staff in hand.

Harry said no more. He shut up.

Whatever about the man behind the desk, Harry wasn't going to make a show of himself in front of Saint Patrick. None of us would have done that.

Mrs O'Leary must have felt happy about the outcome. She would have been sitting there with a smug smile on her face. She'd probably have danced around the room with delight, only now that she was a Councillor she'd have to act the part, look important and all that.

Anyway, once the bit about it only being for the summer was in writing, and our pitch being a Council pitch, we'd have to go along with what was being suggested, not saw down the posts any more, and allow Eddie Marsden to use the pitch. We felt bad about it.

It had always been our pitch, Riverside's pitch. If things had been different we probably wouldn't have minded sharing it, but not with Eddie Marsden.

We weren't into Eddie Marsden. It was like asking Glasgow Rangers and Glasgow Celtic to share the same dressing-room.

No, we didn't like the idea at all.

'Is it true they stoned Saint Patrick?' we asked Harry when we met later outside the Dargle Tavern.

'It's true all right. He was comin' up the Dargle, in off the sea, an' they wouldn't let him land. So he had to shove off an' go somewhere else.'

'Bet I know who stoned him,' suggested Mad Victor.

'Who?'

'Some of Mrs O'Leary's lot.'

'Yeah, some of her ancestors.'

Mrs O'Leary's gang! We all agreed.

3 Things Get Under Way

Chippy came up with a wheelbarrow for selling fruit-'n'-veg. It was a big metal one he was given off a building site. At least he said he was given it. He had to scrape it clean of mortar. Then he sprayed it with red paint. We didn't bother putting a sign on it.

We just left it the way it was. When it was full of carrots, bananas, potatoes and apples, people would soon know what we were at. There was no point in having a squiggly 'fruit-'n'-veg' written on the sides. Once we had the barrow full of the stuff that would be enough.

We painted the wheel and handles black. The black went well with the red, and the barrow looked real nifty. We felt as proud as punch. And it could take a right load, once we were up to shoving it.

Just then we thought of asking Mad Victor to give us a hand. He'd be good at shoving and loading the barrow. Mad Victor was strong as a horse, and we wouldn't have to pay him much. He probably would have done the job for nothing anyway. Apart from the lads who played for Riverside, Mad Victor didn't have any pals, so working on the barrow with us would give him plenty to do. He was only too delighted to give us a hand. He'd have to brush up on his manners though, give up cursing and be nice to the customers.

Chippy gave him a few quick lessons on how to be polite, and all that, and how to weigh the fruit-'n'-veg in plastic bags we got from the supermarkets. But we had to give up on Victor; we couldn't teach him manners. So we got Flintstone McKay to help out instead.

We got a scales, an old pounds and ounces one; the idea was we would weigh up before going out on the road. We sold everything in lbs. We weren't into kilos at all. All the oul' ones loved us for that. They loved talking in lbs and ounces. It brought them back to the old days.

Chippy even got us butchers' aprons to wear. We had straw hats too, only Flintstone's kept falling off from all the running around he was doing. The aprons and hats made us look more business-like, said Chippy.

And of course, everyone on the estate knew us. That meant they all bought off us.

The worst thing about people knowing us was some of them wanted stuff off us on tick.

'What's tick?' Flintstone asked Chippy.

'It's when they haven't any money, and they say they'll pay you later, only they don't.'

'We won't give tick, then?'

'No way. Tick's out. We're not complete fools, ye know.'

Not all our customers wanted tick, only some. Especially those who were into drink and backing horses.

Porky Davis, one of the neighbours, was always after us for tick.

'What d'ye think we are, eejits?' shouted Chippy at him.

'You shouldn't have shouted at him like that, Chippy. He won't buy any more stuff off us.'

'He wouldn't have bought off us anyway,'

scowled Chippy. 'My da says: "Give someone tick an' you don't only lose your money; you lose a customer."'

'How's that?'

'Cause when they owe you money they won't come back. That's how yer customer is lost.'

I wasn't surprised that Chippy would say something like that. Because Chippy is smart, especially with money. Nobody can do him out of money, not even the worse chancers that live around our way.

Business picked up so much we even took in Fassaroe, the housing estate just across from Palermo. It was where Chippy was from. When they saw us wheeling a barrow around the estate they began to call it the 'Hungry Hill Banshee', after Chippy's past antics at the graveyard in Palermo.

Chippy didn't like the name-calling at all. But he turned a deaf ear. He had to. 'The customer is always right,' he'd mutter under his breath.

Pretty soon they were calling the wheel-barrow the 'Hungry Hill Banshee' in Palermo too. Partly because there was a squeak in the wheel. Some oil would have sorted out the squeak, but we decided to put up with it as the name became something of a trade-mark, and we were doing extra business. We even wrote 'Hungry Hill Banshee' on the sides.

Chippy was responsible for buying in fruit 'n' veg. He bought most of it from an uncle of his, Tommy Smith, who drove a Fruit-'n'-Veg lorry for a big Dublin supplier.

'Where does your uncle get it?'

'From the fruit market in Dublin.'

'Is there a big market there?'

'Yeah, near Smithfield.'

'Where's that?'

'Somewhere you wouldn't know. It opens early in the mornin'. My uncle supplies all the shops out this way. An' he gives us the stuff cheaper than the shops get it. An' that means we make more money than the shops. An' we don't have the same overheads.'

'What are overheads?'

'Wages and such like.'

'You don't pay me much,' said Flintstone.

'We do, Flintstone.'

'No you don't. But I don't mind. All I want to do is help.'

Flintstone wasn't the only one who wanted to help. Mad Victor still wanted to give a hand, but we wouldn't let him. Though we bought some fish off him which we sold around the houses. We had no idea where he got it. But, in time, we were to find out. With all the trouble it gave us, I wish we'd known in the first place.

Eddie Marsden moved his Gaelic team on to our pitch in the People's Park. Although we all played Gaelic football at school, none of us would play for Eddie Marsden. We hated him. What we really didn't like was he was always nagging us to play for him. He even came around to the school and tried to persuade the teachers to make us play for him.

'Soccer's a foreign game. You're not real Irishmen if you play soccer.'

'Wha'ye mean, 3-0-3?'

'What's this 3-0-3 business?'

'We'll play what we like. Know what your problem is?'

'What?'

'Ye're a soppy bigot.'

You couldn't talk to Eddie Marsden like that and get away with it. He came yelling after us only he couldn't catch us, especially Flintstone because he could run like a greyhound.

We hadn't called Eddie Marsden a 'soppy bigot'. None of us would have anyway. It was all Mad Victor's fault. He was to blame. *He* was the one who said, 'Ye soppy bigot.' What was more Marsden knew only too well it was Mad Victor and not the rest of us.

He really had it in for Mad Victor after that. Anytime he'd see him he'd glare like hell. It got so bad Victor would cross the road and keep well out of reach. He became afraid of Marsden. Victor was big but Eddie was bigger.

'That Eddie Marsden's a Martian,' he'd say.

'What d'ye mean?'

'Most nights he's peekin' out his window with a telescope, lookin' at the stars.'

'There's nothin' wrong with that, Victor.'

'Nothin' wrong? He's a Martian all right.'

'He's studyin' the stars, that's all.'

'Naw, he's an extra-trest'ial, an' he's always messin' in his garage. I hear noises comin' out.'

'I heard them meself. He's fixin' his car.'

'No, he's an extra-trest'ial. Remember that film *E.T.?* Well he was one. Remember?'

'Yeah. So what?'

'Well, remember when E.T. went to the window and said, "E.T. phone home."?'

'Yeah, sure.'

'Well, that's Eddie Marsden at the window. And the noises in the garage is him tryin' to make a transmitter.'

'Get off it!'

'Know wha' I'm goin' to do?'

'What?'

'Break into his garage and banjax his transmitter.'

'Victor, you'd get into trouble.'

'I wouldn't. Nobody'd know it was me. It could be anybody.'

It took us a while to persuade Mad Victor not to go anywhere near Eddie Marsden's garage, but eventually he gave up on the idea. It was just another of his hair-brained notions – nothing less, nothing more.

What interested us more was what was going on in the Park. True to his word, Eddie Marsden gave Mr Glynn and Harry Hennessy portable goal-posts. They fitted into steel tubing buried in the ground. They were real nifty, though we wouldn't admit as much to Eddie Marsden. We stored them across the road in a garage and they only took a few minutes to put in place.

Harry Hennessy always gave a hand. He told us he used to play in goal for Drumcondra, fat and all as he was. We'd never heard of Drumcondra.

'They used to play in the League of Ireland.

Look at the length of me arms.'

We looked.

They were long all right, all the way down past his knees. And the size of his hands!

They were real big, as big as shovels.

'When ye're big like me, an' got long arms an' big hands, ye can't go wrong as a goal-keeper. Just look.'

We all had another good look at Harry. His arms went way down past his knees. Whatever about being a goalkeeper, he reminded us of a gorilla. A talking one at that.

'King of the goal-mouth, I was.'

The goal-mouth?

King of the jungle, we thought.

4 Harry Hennessy Remembers

The first time they played a Gaelic match on our pitch we went to have a look. Mrs O'Leary was there. She was all over Eddie Marsden, smiling at him, cooing, everything. She even went around patting the kids on the head and giving them sweets out of a big box she had. She gave us none; only dirty looks.

When the match was nearly over, Mr Glynn came along. He shook Eddie Marsden's hand. That really made us mad. We didn't like to see Mr Glynn being friendly with Eddie Marsden. We didn't like it at all. Whatever about Harry Hennessy, he'd stand up to Eddie Marsden. He wouldn't shake his hand. He'd punch him in the face.

Harry was very fond of Mr Glynn. He told us Mr Glynn used to run schoolboy teams in Bray before anybody else did.

'What d'ya mean, Harry?'

'Mr Glynn is a pioneer of soccer in this

town. He ran teams well before soccer was as popular as it is now. He goes back to the days when most people had only radios. He was one of the few who had a telly at home. He fixed it up with a mast, one-hundred-foot high. People had only to look up in the sky to know where George Glynn lived.

'His first team was Field United, named after the field outside his house. In those days there were lots of fields. They're all housing estates now. Every Saturday night George would bring his players around to his house to watch Match-of-the-Day. That's how he got all the kids hooked on soccer.

'Like I said, he was a pioneer. An hour before Match-of-the-Day would start there was a feast of chips, deep-fried by his wife Kay. That's the way it started with George Glynn. Then houses were built on the field opposite him. He moved the lot to the People's Park, changed the name to Riverside Boys, an' that's how you lot got goin'.'

'Ye're not tellin' lies, Harry?'

'No, it's the honest truth.'

Harry was good at telling lies, especially when he had drink taken. But when you got to know him, you knew it wasn't really lies – he believed it all.

He told lies every day, and he drank every day. We always argued over him drinking.

'Harry's a wino.'

'No, he's not. Winos drink wine an' bum money off people. Harry's no bum. An' I've seen him empty a pint glass soon as you'd look away an' turn back again. He's the fastest drinker of Guinness in Bray.'

'Well, he's an alcoholic, then.'

'He's no alcoholic. Real alcoholics only drink whiskey an' spirits. They've no time for Guinness. To be a proper alcoholic ye have to drink whiskey an' spirits.'

'A bottle of whiskey a day,' said Mad Victor. 'Harry's only a drunk. Real alcoholics drink whiskey like they're parched, an' their hands shake all the time.'

'How do you know?'

'Cause me uncles are all alcoholics. An' alcoholics don't fall around the place like

drunks do. They're able to stand up no matter what they drink.'

But we all knew Harry was an alcoholic. It was all over the place that he'd joined Alcoholics Anonymous and they threw him out because he showed up drunk at a meeting. Harry was an alcoholic all right, and he had the belly to prove it.

'Years ago I ran my own football team,' Harry told us while he was going on about Mr

Glynn being a pioneer – a footballing pioneer, that is. 'I ran my own team, Brazil FC I called them. We used to play over at Solus, where they make light bulbs. We had all the Brazil gear, everythin'. Only we didn't play like Brazil, we played like us – win a match one week, lose a match, that kinda team. We nearly got runners-up in the League once. Then it all folded.'

'How did that happen, Harry?'

'I used to collect fifty pence a head off the players after every match. We had a row over that. The money was to pay the ref's match-fee, but lads said I was drinkin' it. So they did the dirt on me. Some of them began to walk off the pitch before the match'd be over an' scarper without payin' me the fifty pence. We became financially embarrassed.'

'Wha's that, Harry?'

'Fin-an-cially em-barr-assed.'

'Like when ye're caught nickin' somethin'?'

'No, the team went broke. I did away with the team. Then I took up refereein'. Now this, helpin' out with you lot.'

After hearing Harry Hennessy telling us all about him and Mr Glynn, and how Riverside Boys became a football club, we knew we were part of a proud tradition, part of a chunk of history, more than could be said for Eddie and Margo Marsden, and Mrs O'Leary for that matter.

There was more to Riverside Boys than the three of them put together.

Riverside Boys were there long before Mrs O'Leary ever got involved. And, according to Harry Hennessy, long before Eddie Marsden and Margo knew how to push a pram, or before they started their own GAA team.

I said that to Margo, one day I met her in Quinnsworth. All I got was a clip around the ear, and a chase down the aisle, between the breakfast cereals and the tinned fruit.

I shouted it at her when I got to the door, too. Everybody looked, and she was hopping mad. I think I gave her a bad name.

At least, I hope I did

5 Fishy!

Early that summer my dad had bought a new car. Well, not exactly new. It was an old one, but if you polished it it shone like new.

'It's a Ford Capri,' he had said. 'Bought it for six hundred quid. A bargain. They wanted a thou but I knocked them down to six hundred. We'll be able to go to Brittas Bay every Sunday. It'll be great for the summer.'

I looked the car over. There was plenty of room. We wouldn't have to take turns going to Brittas Bay. We'd all fit in together, no bother. All we needed was some good weather.

'Where did you get the money for the car, Da?'

'What d'ye mean?'

'You never have any money, Da. Not real money. Not six hundred pounds in one go.'

'I had some good wins on the horses lately. Don't tell yer ma that. She thinks it's money that was owed off a job.'

Da is a betting man. He'd bet on two flies climbing up a wall. Usually, when he went out, Ma would make him empty his pockets first. She had a rule – he was never allowed out with more than £3 in his pocket at a time. We weren't supposed to know, because if we did it might have made him feel bad. But we knew, and more than that. He usually hid money in a tin can and kept it in a hole in the garden wall. He is real daft, my da – real daft.

The car turned out a waste of money. It was grand the first few times, but after that we had to shove it down the road to get it going. You'd be up the town and it would break down. It'd only take two minutes to get up the town, then it'd conk out. Da would spend ages trying to fix it, either that or halt someone he knew to get a tow back home.

After a few weeks we all got fed up with the Ford Capri. But Da kept it anyway. He used it as a kind of room he'd go into and read the paper.

'It'll save us buildin' on to the house,' he said.

But he wasn't fooling us. There was no way he was going to build on to the house. Anyway, nobody would buy the car off him. He was stuck with it.

Sometimes me and Chippy used the car. We had a ghetto-blaster. The car was good for that. We'd go out to the car and turn the ghetto-blaster on and let on we were going somewhere.

That's the way we were. We were good at letting on.

I knew there was something wrong with the fish Mad Victor was selling us. It smelled more than it should have. Some of the people we were selling the fish to began to complain. They weren't too keen to buy it. The way things ended up we weren't too keen either.

We found out that Mad Victor was going into fish shops, giving the poor mouth about him and his little brother, Mad Henry, starving, and getting leftover fish because the fishmongers felt sorry for him. He sold most of it to us, and it was only afterwards that we found out there was something wrong with it.

The way it came about was like this: Midge Baker, an oul' one with a rottweiler dog, was rushed to hospital one night.

We were playing football on the road outside her house. Next thing, an ambulance came speeding up the road and screeched to a halt outside her door. The ambulance men went into the house and took her out on a kind of chair-stretcher. The rottweiler got into the ambulance with her. The ambulance men were afraid of the rottweiler and they didn't know what to do. Only for Mad Victor they wouldn't have been able to get him out of the ambulance. He had a way with dogs and he got the rottweiler out, no bother.

What we saw of Midge, she looked as pale as a sheet.

'Food-poisoning,' we heard the ambulance men say.

'Is she goin' to die?' asked Flintstone.

'Course not,' said one of the ambulance men. 'We'll bring her into hospital, pump her out, and she'll be as right as rain.'

This time it was Mad Victor's turn to ask a stupid question.

'Is that what they do in hospitals?'

The ambulance men didn't bother answering Mad Victor, not at first.

'Who's going to look after the dog?'

Look after the dog? Neither me, Chippy nor Flintstone would look after the dog. It was too fierce.

'I'll look after it,' said Mad Victor.

'Where'll you keep it?'

'In me bedroom.'

'You won't be allowed.'

What the ambulance men didn't know was Mad Victor could do what he liked. There was no one to stop him, except his uncles, and they were nearly always too drunk to know what was going on. It was no bother for Mad Victor to keep a rottweiler in his bedroom. He could have kept an elephant in there and his uncles wouldn't have been any the wiser.

At the time, we'd no idea how Midge got a bout of food-poisoning. Though we knew she was in real pain. Maybe they'd operate and patch up her stomach. Maybe even give her a new one. But we knew she couldn't be given a new stomach. Even Mad Victor knew that.

Once the ambulance left, however, we were more intent on bringing Midge's rottweiler back to Mad Victor's house.

We didn't know his name, so we decided to call him Jaws. Mad Victor took his belt off and used it as a lead, But even though he coaxed it most of the way, it was tough going. Luckily a cat shot through the gate of Victor's house and that got it the rest of the way.

It was a few days later, when we went down to the Park for a kick-about, that we found out how Midge Baker got food-poisoning.

'Lads,' said Mad Victor, 'I think I know how Midge got poisoned.'

'What d'ye mean?'

'Well, some of the fish you sold Midge was oul' stuff I got for nothin'. I didn't think it'd poison her though.'

'Why did you sell it to us then?'

'For money, that's why.'

'Half the estate coulda got poisoned. There coulda been twenty ambulances up there takin' people away. You coulda ruined the whole thing on us.'

Luckily, for us, Midge was the only one who got food-poisoning. She was back out of hospital inside a week. There wasn't a bother out of her. I don't think she even remembered the fish. But we remembered. We wouldn't buy any more fish from Victor.

He brought Midge's rottweiler back to her soon as she got out of hospital. But not before he brought him off hunting.

'What were you and Jaws huntin' for,' we asked him. 'Rabbits?'

'Naw, drug-pushers.'

6 An Explosive Affair

Mrs O'Leary was beginning to throw her weight about at the local Council meetings – they always had a monthly meeting in the Town Hall on the first Tuesday of the month.

The Councillors never did much; just went to meetings to talk and that. They had a big table that they sat around. It was as long as a house and, depending where you sat, you had to shout to be heard. It suited Mrs O'Leary just fine as she was never done shouting. And they were always banging their fists on the table. Only Mrs O'Leary didn't bang her fist; she thumped her handbag. The nearest Councillor was lucky if he didn't get thumped too.

Sometimes the public could go and listen to them, though there wasn't much room for the public. Whether there was room or not didn't really matter, because you only had to stand outside on the stairs to hear what was going on. The staircase was very big; it could hold about sixty people. Not that sixty people in Bray wanted to hear what was going on, because nothing really went on anyway, except shouting and banging the table, and saying the opposite to what was being proposed.

How did I know all this?

I knew because there was a section in the local paper dealing with Council meetings. Mrs O'Leary got a mention most weeks. Once she wanted the Council to build a bridge across the river Dargle only yards from our

football pitch. But, luckily, the rest of the Council didn't want to go ahead with the idea as there were no funds. Our Council is nearly always broke.

Mrs O'Leary came up with loads of other stupid proposals. She gave out about the dogs in the town, said there were too many of them. She wanted all dogs without a collar rounded up and sent to somewhere in County Wicklow to a Dogs' Home.

That caused problems for most of us who played for Riverside. We nearly all had dogs, except for me. Mad Victor had four dogs, Flintstone McKay two. Chippy even had a dog, and Harry Hennessy was thinking of getting one (mainly to take him safely home after the pubs closed at night). Apart from the dogs we had, there were loads of dogs on our estate, and only a few had collars.

'What'll we do about the dogs?' asked Mad Victor. 'They'll take them all to the Dogs' Home and put them down.'

'They won't. Why d'ye think it's called the Dogs' *Home?* They'll look after them.'

'No, they won't. If they can't find homes in a week or two they put them down.'

'They can't do that. It's murder!'

'Well, that's what they do. Only I'm goin' to do somethin' about it. They'll take no dogs off this estate. I'll make sure that they don't.'

'How'll ye do that?'

'I'll go to the pet-shops, nick a load of dog-collars, an' put them on the dogs.'

And that was what Mad Victor did. He visited the two pet-shops in town and lifted loads of collars. After a few weeks every dog in our estate had a collar. One of the shops almost closed for good. But not quite. People whose dogs lost their collars got into the habit of buying a new one, and buying other stuff as well. So, in the end, Mad Victor was really the shops' best friend.

Mrs O'Leary tried to get the Council to do lots of other things, too. She got the Council, and those in other towns, to sponsor a nationwide Gaelic football tournament. Eddie Marsden and Margo were to manage the Bray entry. We didn't pay much heed at first, but just after everyone agreed to Mrs O'Leary's suggestion something happened that made us change our minds. We were all mad keen to mess it up in the end.

What happened was: Mad Victor knew this lad who went to our school. He was a good few years older than us, and was in Sixth Year. His name was 'Brains' O'Mahony. He was real clever. Cleverer than the teachers.

There's a sand-pit across the fields from Fassaroe, where Mad Victor used to go. He thought Apaches lived there, and he wanted to join up and become one of them. He wanted to live like Geronimo and have a horse, and go into Bray and shoot off a load of arrows and run Mrs O'Leary out of town.

One day he came across Brains O'Mahony in the quarry.

Brains asked him for a match.

'Wha' d'ye want a match for?'

'I want to set this off.'

'Wha' is it?'

Mad Victor had to ask, because whatever it was Brains wanted to set off was wrapped in paper. When Brains took the paper off Mad Victor could see it was a three-foot rocket.

'That's a rocket, ain't it?'

'A prototype.'

'A wha'?'

'It's a test-rocket. The real thing's back home. I'm only testin' it to see if my idea works.'

'You mean ye've got a bigger one. Where's it goin' to, the moon?'

'Don't be daft. I'm only equating velocities.'

'Wha'?' Mad Victor didn't press the point. Probably figured he wouldn't understand the answer either.

'Have you got a match?'

Luckily, Mad Victor had one. He couldn't understand how Brains was clever enough to make a rocket, and at the same time stupid enough to forget to bring matches to set if off.

'You're a kind of professor, aren't ye?'

'What do you mean?'

'Well, to make a rocket you have to be a professor. Only professors can make rockets.'

Brains O'Mahony didn't bother to answer. He took the box of matches from Mad Victor, ferried the rocket on to a rock base, and told Victor to stand well back. He lit the fuse and ran behind a boulder. The fuse sizzled in a coloured flashing. Next thing, the rocket took off and disappeared over the brow of the sand-pit.

Mad Victor was very impressed with Brains and the rocket. He followed him all the way across the fields, back into Bray where Brains lived. Seemingly, Brains had a workshop in a shed at the bottom of his garden. Mad Victor was real keen to see inside but Brains wouldn't let him in.

Mad Victor wasn't offended. 'Don't forget, if ye ever make a real rocket, an' want a spaceman to go in it, I'll be yer spaceman.'

Brains didn't jump at the offer. But he met up with Mad Victor quite a bit after that. Mad Victor used to carry his bits and pieces up to the sand-pits and give him a hand that way. Brains had a lot of stuff that needed to be carried about, and he was only too glad of some help, once Victor kept his mouth shut and kept their secret. And he needn't have worried. Mad Victor was well able to keep a secret. He even stood in front of Brains and swore in the name of Geronimo he'd say nothing to anyone.

Two weeks later Brains decided to test his main rocket. On account of it being so big, he got in touch with Mad Victor to give a hand carrying it. Also, as the sand-pits were a long way from his house, he decided to launch the rocket from the Back Strand, which was near enough to where he lived. They wouldn't have too far to carry the rocket.

So early on a Sunday morning, when there was no one around, they set the rocket up on the beach, ignited it and, lo and behold! it blasted off straight into a cliff. The front of the cliff collapsed in a heap, just missing Brains and Mad Victor by inches.

The explosion was heard all over Bray. Within minutes squad-cars were racing to the Back Stand. There were policemen all over the place. Poor Victor got caught, dust and sand all over him. Only when they rubbed it off did they know it was him.

'It's not you again?' they said.

'Course it's me again.'

'We should have known.'

'That's right, ye shoulda known.'

Mad Victor was put in the back of a squad-car and taken to the Garda Station.

Brains wasn't found for another five or ten minutes. He was lying in a pile of seaweed, flat out. He wasn't hurt badly, though. They took him to hospital and kept him in to check he didn't conk out. It was the end of his rockets and workshop though. The Gardai took the lot away in a lorry.

As for Mad Victor, the Gardai didn't charge him.

At the next Council meeting Mrs O'Leary, shouting and thumping the handbag, kicked up about the explosion.

Next thing was she got in touch with the Eastern Health Board. A car was sent around to Mad Victor's house. He and his brother Mad Henry were put in the car and placed in care.

We felt gutted about what had happened – and it was all Mrs O'Leary's doing. She had told the Eastern Health Board that Victor and Henry's uncles weren't capable of looking after them, and that was why they were taken away and placed in care.

We decided to get our own back on her. And as she was the brains behind the new Gaelic football event, we decided to wreck it.

How?

We would join Eddie Marsden's team and hope to cause enough hassle to get her into trouble.

And how would that come about?

By telling a little white lie and doing a bit of cheating.

We didn't mind telling lies once it got Mrs O'Leary into trouble. We didn't mind cheating either, because that'd definitely get her into trouble.

Once there was trouble for Mrs O'Leary, we'd be happy.

Very happy.

So we told lies and joined Eddie Marsden's team.

Once on the team, we cheated a lot. Every match, to be exact. We could hardly wait for the trouble to start.

7 A Plot is Hatched

It wasn't easy for us to come to terms with the idea of playing Gaelic football for Eddie Marsden and Margo. But if, as a result, Mrs O'Leary got into trouble, the turnaround would be acceptable.

Flintstone McKay couldn't understand how playing for Eddie Marsden could get her into trouble. So we had to explain it to him, slowly.

'It's like this, Flintstone. The competition is for U-13s. If we sign on an' do well they'll want to see our birth-certs.'

'But we're U-14s. We're over age.'

'That's it. Mrs O'Leary is in charge of all the birth-certs. We won't give any at first. We'll hold out as long as we can. Then, when we give the birth-certs an, the committee finds out, there'll be holy murder an' they'll eat the head off Mrs O'Leary for lettin' us play.'

'But some of the lads that play for Eddie Marsden know we're over age. They'll tell him.'

'No, they won't. Cause if they do we'll burst 'em. Then, once we win, it won't matter if they tell, cause Mrs O'Leary, on account of bein' in charge of the birth-certs, will be in big trouble, an' we won't care once she's in trouble.'

Flintstone was impressed. 'Brill!'

'It *is* brill,'

'And you thought it up?'

'No... Brains O'Mahony had the idea. He said it'd work an' all, once we held the birth-certs back a while, an' won a few matches. He's dead brill, is Brains. He says it'll get her into big trouble, cause she's on the committee of this thing. It'll be great. An' know what?'

'Wha'?'

'We'll get to see most of Ireland, travellin' to matches an' all that. It'll be better than playin' for Riverside an' only goin' around Dublin. We might be goin' to places like Kerry, even Donegal, real faraway places. It'll be deadly. An' if we like it we can go missin' an' not come back. We could let Mrs O'Leary take the blame for that too. By the time we're finished she'll be sorry she ever sent Mad Victor to a rotten oul' home for orphans.'

She'd be sorry, all right.

We'd definitely get our own back for what she did to Mad Victor.

When we joined Eddie Marsden's Gaelic team we thought he'd be delighted to have all us great footballers playing for him.

But he wasn't.

'After all the hard time you lot have been giving me with the goal-posts why, all of a sudden, do you want to play football for me?'

'Cause we want to. We're Irish, ye know. We can play Gaelic football if we want to.'

It was sick-making having to go down to the Park and see those two giant goal-posts looming over *our* soccer pitch. It still hurt like hell to see them there, but we did our best to hide our feelings. We thought of poor Victor in some children's home, some big grim building with wooden benches in it. And he'd have to queue with a bowl, like in the film *Oliver Twist,* and ask for more porridge.

'Gimme more! Gimme more!'

And Mad Henry'd ask for more too.

And all they'd get would be a clip on the ear and be told to go back down and sit on the hard bench.

It wasn't easy putting on an act in front of Eddie Marsden, letting on that all of a sudden we liked him. And then there was Margo, cooing like a daft pigeon, telling us what great fellows we were playing Gaelic football, and that one day we'd grow up to be like Padraig Pearse and James Connolly, and that we'd be a credit to the country, as if we weren't going to be that anyway.

That woman made me sick. It wasn't easy putting up with her. She knew nothing about Gaelic football. The only thing she knew about was history. It was all she could go on about. She was dead nuts about history, James Connolly in particular.

'You could all grow up to be like James Connolly,' she said for the umpteenth time.

'We don't want to grow up to be like James Connolly, Margo. We don't want to be carried out, put in a chair and shot. We're not that daft.'

And we weren't.

We hadn't the guts to be patriots.

We had brains, and we intended to use them to get our own back on Mrs O'Leary.

Mrs O'Leary came to the pitch and told us about the details of the competition.

'You'll have to play some matches locally,' she said, 'and if you win you'll have to play the winners of outside areas, and if you win them you get to play in the finals at Croke Park.'

The idea of playing in Croke Park appealed to us. We had seen it often enough on telly. And anything we saw on telly we were dead keen on.

'You'll have to have your birth-certs. The competition is U-13. Your birth-certs have to be handed in to me, as proof of being the right age. You're all U-13, aren't you?'

'Yes,' we lied.

We'd already had a word with the lads on Marsden's regular Gaelic team who knew we were over age. We told them to keep their mouths shut or Mad Victor would escape from wherever he was locked up by the social workers and belt them. They were all terrified of Mad Victor.

'An' if he escapes he'll be meaner an' worse than ever he was, cause wherever he is they're real cruel to him, an' that'll make him madder. If he escapes an' you tell Mrs O'Leary we're over age, he'll come after you, an' it'll be like a

nightmare. Only it won't be Frankenstein, it'll be Mad Victor, an' it'll be worse than any nightmare, worse than anythin' you've seen in *Nightmare on Elm Street*.'

That really got to them. There was no way they were going to tell Mrs O'Leary, or Eddie Marsden, that we were over age.

'Don't forget your birth-certs. At the latest, I want them before you play the other county winners.'

'We'll have them, Mrs O'Leary. We'll have them.'

But we had no intention of doing things the way Mrs O'Leary wanted us to. She was an old bag, a raving tyrant, as far as we were concerned. We'd hold out on the birth-certs as long as we could. With a bit of luck we'd do well in the competition, maybe get to the final in Croke Park before we'd be found out.

We fancied we'd do well in the competition, because most of us were good Gaelic football players. We were all on the school team. As usual Chippy was the star. He played centre-field. I played right-half-forward. Flintstone played top-of-the-left. Two of the others played centre-back and left-half-forward.

And that was it.

We fancied our chances all right.

Then the birth-certs would show up.

That, we were really looking forward to.

8 Eddie Ned

I heard something interesting from Ma last night. Well, it was interesting but a bit embarrassing at the same time. Ma is great for family history. She is always telling me about bits of things that happened years ago. Ma loves talking about ordinary, everyday things. She just loves *Coronation Street.*

Getting back to Ma talking about years ago, she told me how my da's granda got his name. Not that I was bothered, but she was bursting at the seams to tell me anyway.

'Know how your da's granda got his name?'

'No. What was his name?'

'Eddie Ned.'

'That's short for Edward, isn't it, Ma?'

'Suppose it is. But there was no one in the family ever called Edward before.'

'Why did they call him Eddie Ned then?'

'They had a donkey called Eddie Ned. They called him after the donkey. They wanted to carry the name on.'

'Why didn't they just get another donkey?'

'Did you ever hear your da's granda laugh?'

'Course not. That would have been years ago.'

'Well, if you had heard him laugh you'd know why they called him after the donkey.'

'Why, Ma?'

'Cause he had a laugh like a donkey's bray. His own da was like that too, and his granda. It passed on.'

'You're jokin', Ma?'

'Course not, I'm bein' honest. As honest as the stars in the sky.'

'How come it never came out in the family since?'

'Don't ask silly questions. Count yourself lucky.'

And I was counting myself lucky. Who'd want a laugh like a donkey? Somebody wouldn't be lucky though. It would come out in the family some day. Now that I knew, I wished my da had been born with a laugh like a donkey's bray.

I didn't hate my da, I just disliked him.

Why?

I don't know really.

It was just inside me, part of me I guess.

Maybe, like Da's grandad's laugh, it was something passed down through the family.

Maybe.

One night, me and the rest of the family were watching telly. Something made Da laugh. It wasn't an ordinary laugh. It was real deep, like it travelled from way down inside his belly. Ma couldn't believe her ears.

'That laugh, it's just like your granda's,' she said to Da.

'How could it?' he answered.

'Well, I'm tellin' you now. It's just like your granda's.'

Then Da laughed again.

You could see Ma and my two sisters felt mortified.

'I'm laughin' like him all right. Fifty-four years of age an' now all of a sudden I'm laughin' like a donkey. How's that? Why has it

happened to me?'

As for me, I was delighted.

All that worried me was maybe it would happen to me when I got to be fifty-four. I wouldn't want that. Imagine laughing like a donkey? You'd be afraid to go anywhere for fear of making a show of yourself.

As for Da, once he kept that laugh up, I'd bring him anywhere there was a crowd. Anywhere that'd make a show of him.

'That's me da. He laughs like a donkey'.

'What's that you said, Jimmy?'

'Nothin', Ma... Just thinkin'.'

'Well, don't. Not like that, anyway.'

As for Da, Ma took him to the doctor next day.

'I can do nothing for you,' the doctor said.

'Nothin'?' asked my da, sodden-eyed.

'No, nothing.'

Both Ma and Da were heart-broken.

Me, I was double-delighted.

9 We Do a Deal

The first match we played for Eddie Marsden in Mrs O'Leary's National Gaelic Football Tournament was at home against Greystones, right on our soccer pitch. We still felt bad about getting out on the pitch and playing for Eddie Marsden and Margo. It was strange with him wandering up and down the sideline telling us what to do. The only ones we were ever used to on the sideline were Mr Glynn and Harry Hennessy.

Before the game against Greystones began we complained to Mrs O'Leary. We felt Greystones shouldn't be in the competition.

'Mrs O'Leary, Greystones ain't got an Urban Council, they shouldn't be in the competition.'

'Of course, they have a Council.'

'It's not a Council, Mrs O'Leary, it's a Town Commission. There's a difference.'

And there was a difference. At least, the name was different. We knew only too well there was no Urban Council in Greystones. There was nothing, only a Town Commission, whatever that was.

'Mrs O'Leary, the rules say only places with local Councils can play. You made the rules, you should know.'

But Mrs O'Leary wouldn't hear of Greystones not being allowed to play against us.

'It's all about sport. And sport is all about participation,' she went on.

She'd know what sport was all about when she got a hand on our birth-certs. None of us had brought them to her so far. If she wanted birth-certs she'd have to burgle our houses.

But there was another reason why we didn't want to play Greystones.

'See that skinny lad there?'

'Yer man?'

'An' that lad with the squinty eyes?'

'Wha' about him?'

'An' yer man with the Chelsea football bag?'

'He has a stutter, hasn't he?'

'Sure. You recognise them now, don't ye?'

'They all play for Shamrock Boys, don't they?' Shamrock Boys were our soccer rivals.

'Yeah, an' soon as we get out on that pitch they're goin' to recognise us. An' as soon as they recognise us they're goin' to know we're over age.'

'You're forgettin' one thing though.'

'What?'

'They're probably over age themselves.'

I'd never thought of that. Trust Chippy. He probably was right. Well, if they played our age group in soccer, they must have been over age. Well, they'd hardly be all under age when we were over age.

Just then Chippy had an idea and called the three Greystones players in behind one of the trees at the side of the pitch.

'Lads, it's like this…'

'Like what?'

'We know ye three are over age…'

'We're not! Ye lot are!'

Still Chippy went on. 'We want no trouble, do we? You don't want trouble. We don't want trouble. That bein' the case, we can come to an agreement. Are ye on?'

'What kind of agreement?'

'If ye win we say nothin'. If we win ye say nothin'.'

The Greystones lads didn't bother answering, but it wasn't because they were shy. Chippy still had to do the talking.

'Do ye like fruit?'

'What kind?'

'Apples? Bananas?'

'Grapes?' I added.

The Greystones lads couldn't see the connection between us and fruit. But we could. We had a load left over. Not that business was bad; it was booming. We had bought too much in, that was all. If the Greystones lads would be willing to take the overload, we'd be only too willing to hand it over. Anything to keep the peace and stay in Mrs O'Leary's Gaelic football competition another while.

'We'll take it.'

'Good.'

'Have ye any coconuts to throw in?'

'No, they don't eat coconuts up our way.

Would a melon do?'

'What's that?'

'A big green thing.'

'No, thanks. We'll take the rest though.'

'Done?'

'Done.'

One of the Greystones lads spat on the palm of his hand and shook hands with Chippy. He must have been a farmer's son from outside Greystones, because farmers always spit on their hands before doing a deal. Well, they did in the old days. And the old days weren't too far away from Greystones.

We did the business on the pitch too. Mrs O'Leary, Eddie Marsden and Margo were all delighted. We won, no bother. All that had to be done was to give the Greystones lads some fruit. We brought it down to the Park after Mrs O'Leary, Eddie Marsden and all left.

You'd think there was famine in Greystones. The whole team was there waiting for a share. They stuffed their football bags, their pockets, even their mouths, with the stuff. They emptied the complete barrow load. We began

to think they'd look for more, not that they were going to get any more. But they plodded off up the Park to get the bus home to Greystones, leaving a trail of apple-butts and banana skins behind them.

But fair play, they never once mentioned we were over age. Mrs O'Leary would have to wait a little longer to find that out. And when she did, we could hardly wait to see the look on her face. It would be well worth seeing.

Maybe even better than getting to the final in Croke Park.

I'm sitting here in the box-room, thinking what might have been with *Forlorn Love*, the story no one believed I'd written, the one that had gone missing, the one I would have won the book competition with.

The sun is setting outside. You can't see it from my window, not directly. But if I stick my head out of the window and look to the left I can see it all right. I like looking at the sun setting. I like looking at the sea too – even mountains. If you're into that kind of thing it means you're something of a poet. You'd have no bother writing poetry. All you'd need is the inspiration – a little shove to set you off writing like mad. And you have to be mad to write poetry, just look at the stuff that's written. All poets are mad. Some even get put away, just like Mad Victor and Mad Henry.

Sometimes I write poems, especially nasty ones about my da. I'm not really into writing poetry though. Not because I don't like it, but because I'm afraid I'll end up nuts. That's why I'd rather write stories, You don't go barmy if you write stories. But if you write poetry you definitely go nuts. They all do.

Once we had a poet who lived on our road. He'd spend all day writing poems. Writing poems and going for long walks on his own. When you met him you couldn't even say hello or he'd turn on you.

'Don't talk. Stay quiet. I'm thinkin' up a poem.'

'How was I to know? I was only tryin' to be friendly.'

'Don't then. Friends are really enemies. They get in the way of the creative process.'

I liked that, the creative process bit. I used the phrase now and again to try and impress Heather McFadden, my ex-girlfriend. But she'd have none of it, just told me to shove off. She thinks I'm some kind of creep. I'm beginning to believe her.

Well, I'm not really. But when I sometimes recite my poems in public, and keep going on about Robert Browning (that's the name a few of us thought up for Ray Parker, the fellow on our estate who's into poetry), how could anyone not think I was a creep?

And another reason why.

I spend a lot of time on my own in the box-room. You have to if you want to be a writer. You have to sit down for hours on your own, maybe go for walks on your own. Just like Robert Browning does. Next thing you can end up talking to yourself. Luckily, I don't talk to myself, not a lot anyway. Robert Browning talks to himself. He talks to himself all the time. Either that, or he just shuts up completely.

The night after we played Greystones in the Park, Robert Browning went around the estate reciting poems through the neighbours' letter-boxes. His ma went out and tried to get him to give up the reciting and come home.

But he wouldn't.

He went on and on.

The whole road got poetry. Poetry, poetry and more poetry.

Like I said, his ma had to go into the house without him. He stayed out all night and went to live in the bushes on the side of Bray Head. He writes a lot of poems on Bray Head, and he comes down into the town every third or fourth day, and recites his new poems in the middle of Main Street.

He still does. Only I know what's going to happen to him. An ambulance will come along and grab him. He'll be brought off to the nut-house, and that'll be the end of Robert Browning, poems and all.

Writing can be a dangerous game – your mind can snap, just like Robert Browning's. I won't turn out like Robert Browning though. When you play for Riverside Boys you have to have plenty of cop-on, and I've lots of that.

No, there's no way I'll ever turn out like Robert Browning.

No, sir-ee!

10 Away to Wicklow

Our next game in Mrs O'Leary's tournament was away to Wicklow. Eddie Marsden told us to meet at 1.30 pm at the bottom of the Dargle Road. The match was due to start at 3 o'clock, so we had plenty of time to spare.

Chippy, Flintstone, myself and the rest of the Riverside lads showed up a bit late on purpose. We wanted Eddie Marsden to sweat a while, make him think we weren't going to show up at all.

We hung around in a side street, up the road from where Eddie Marsden and the team were waiting. They were sitting patiently in a minibus, with the doors open, waiting for us to arrive. After a while Eddie Marsden got out, kept on looking up the road, checking his watch, getting more and more anxious by the minute.

Every now and again we'd have a squint around the corner to make sure the minibus wouldn't go without us.

Chippy did most of the squinting.

While we were waiting, one of the lads came up with something really cool.

'You know how Mrs O'Leary wants our birth-certs?'

'Well, we're handin' over nothin'. Why should we, when we're all over age? Let her find out the hard way.'

'I was just thinkin',' continued the lad with the bright idea. 'I might give her me baptismal cert, cause I wasn't baptised until I was three, an' that'd put me well under age.'

'How did it take that long? Were you lost, or somethin'?'

'No. I was born in England. Me ma says there's no churches in England, that they're all pagans. I had to wait until we came home to Ireland.'

'Of course there's churches in England. England's full of churches. They even have mosques in England.'

'Mosques? What are they?'

'They're Moslem churches. There's that

many Moslems in England that pretty soon they'll be replacin' horses with camels for all the Moslems to go around on.'

'Think I should give me baptismal to Mrs O'Leary?'

'No, let her go to pot.'

'Hey, we better hurry. Eddie Marsden's gettin' into the minibus. I think it's goin' to go without us.'

We ran around the corner as quick as we could. In the end we were in a mad rush to get to the minibus. It pulled out a few yards, probably on purpose, wanting us to run that little bit extra. But we got there. Flintstone, as usual, was first.

We trampled all over the other lads in the minibus, and made room for ourselves. We kept quiet all the way to Wicklow but that didn't mean we were going to stay quiet. We were saving up the fun for afterwards.

Wicklow were a good team. But we were better. They acted kind of friendly, but on account of never having seen them before we weren't in any humour to be friendly. So we just got stuck into them, and beat the lard out of them, as much as the ref would allow. We were good at that – good at going to the edge and just stopping in time so as not to get sent off.

Maybe it would have been different if we had known the Wicklow lads from before, but we didn't. So we got stuck into them and acted real mean. I think that's what Eddie Marsden wanted anyway, because he didn't give out. He didn't tell us to stop what we were going on with. I don't think he minded at all, once we won.

And we did win. Now we were into the next round. But we weren't thinking of the next match, or the one we'd just played. Soon as we got changed we made for the shops.

We intended to load up with Mars bars, Snickers, chocolate, lollipops, everything. But the people in the shops saw us coming, shoved us outside, and locked the doors.

We were starving all the way back to Bray. All we got was a Kit-Kat and Chippy ate that.

Eddie Marsden gave out like hell, but we didn't care. When we got back to Bray he

phoned Mrs O'Leary to tell her we'd won. He said she was delighted. She had gone over to Manchester for the wedding of one of her nieces. But like us coming home from Wicklow, she ended up starving.

So Flintstone McKay said, because one of his uncles was over at the wedding. All that there was to eat at the reception was a few sandwiches. It was the most miserable wedding ever. There were about forty guests and fifteen sandwiches, so Flintstone McKay said. And it was must have been the truth, because Flintstone never lies.

I wrote to the crowd that's holding the book competition. I told them all about what happened to *Forlorn Love.* I asked them could they send me an invitation to the reception when they'd be announcing the winner. They said they would, but not until it got nearer the time.

The letter made my day. I decided that when I got the invitation I'd get my sisters to frame it. I'd keep it in the box-room, right next to the table I do all my writing on. It would keep me in the humour to write, maybe even inspire me.

Talking about writing, sometimes when I'm writing, my eyes get sore. I think it's from looking at all the white paper.

I had a good chat with Brains O'Mahony about it. You can talk to Brains – he doesn't slag. He takes it all in and offers good advice.

'Brains, how come sometimes when I'm writin' the white of the paper makes me eyes sore?'

'That's only natural. It happens all the time.'

'What d'you mean?'

'Well, if you look at anything white long enough it's bound to make your eyes sore. Did you ever think why grass is green?'

'No.'

'Well, God made it that way. Because green is easy on the eyes. You can look at grass all day an' your eyes never get sore. Think you could do that if grass was white?'

'You mean, when I'm writin' I should use green paper?'

'Not necessarily. What I'm saying is, green is easy on the eyes. It doesn't harm them.'

I kind of knew what Brains was talking about. Brains is dead clever. That's what I like about him most. He knows everything. Fancy knowing about green being soothing on the eyes. Only someone like Brains would know that.

Anyway, I wrote a kind of poem about my da. He's a desert – completely empty. I don't want to explain, but if you ever met my da you'd understand.

It's called 'The Labour Man'.

My da
Is a man
Whose name
Is known
At the Labour Exchange.

His name
Is always there,
Squashed
In the middle
Of a computer file.

My da,
First
In the door,
And
Last in the queue.

My da: The Labour Man.

11 The Bubble Bursts

We won our next few Gaelic matches. Chippy was dead nifty off frees, and I scored a few goals. Flintstone McKay even got in on the act. At soccer he could never score. But he was always good at putting the ball over the bar, and in Gaelic that mattered.

Mrs O'Leary went to all the matches. She always made her family and relations attend as well. The complete pitch was encircled by O'Learys and they'd wear the team colours and shout themselves hoarse.

When we played at home, what with all the O'Learys shouting and jumping up and down like African tribesmen, the other team was usually frightened out of its wits. It was much worse than when we played at home for Riverside Boys. Then we only had Harry Hennessy, Mr Glynn and a few strays to cheer us on. With Mrs O'Leary's lot it was like having Hill 16 behind you, only more furious, even more deadly.

It didn't take us long to carve up the other teams in Wicklow. Then it was on to the other counties. First we beat a team from Wexford, then a team from Louth. Meanwhile Mrs O'Leary was pestering us full-time for our birth-certs. Everybody else had their certs in at least a month. But we, the Riverside players, were a complete blank as far as they were concerned.

But we didn't care, especially me, Chippy and Flintstone. What was more, we had plenty of money to spend from our fruit 'n' veg round. That made our trips around the country all the more enjoyable. In the end, we couldn't wait to go off and play another match we were having that much of a good time.

Then the bubble burst, and Mrs O'Leary's dream began to turn into a nightmare.

When we were playing a team from Portlaoise in the Park in the quarter-finals, Chippy scored a great goal. He soloed the ball half the length of the pitch, dodging in and out through the Portlaoise team, and planted the ball right in the corner of the net.

It was a wonder goal. All the O'Learys went mad, jumping up and down on the sideline, and Margo ran out on the pitch and planted a big wet kiss on Chippy's lips. He hated that. But it didn't put him off his stride. He followed it up with another great goal and two well-taken points.

We flattened Portlaoise. Only, after the game someone told Mrs O'Leary that Chippy was over age. She blew her top. Took him to one side and nagged him until he admitted he was the wrong age.

That finished Chippy on the team.

Mrs O'Leary came down like a ton of bricks on the Riverside players that were left. We had to produce our birth-certs before the next match.

We were a bit sore about that, because the next match was the semi-final and if we won we'd be in the final at Croke Park. And as much as we disliked Mrs O'Leary, Eddie Marsden and Margo, we all wanted to play in Croke Park. It would have been nearly as good as playing for Ireland at soccer. We definitely had our hearts set on playing in Croke Park. All of a sudden, it was our life ambition.

But Mrs O'Leary stopped us.

The semi-final was to be played in Longford against a team from there. We were to go by luxury coach. Harry Hennessy got wind of the trip. He was fed up drinking in Bray so he thought he'd go for a day's outing and see what the pubs in Longford were like.

Mrs O'Leary was waiting for us and as soon as we got near the bus she said, 'Where's your birth-certs?'

'In our pockets, Mrs O'Leary.'

'Show them to me?'

'Mrs O'Leary, ye'll only slow everyone gettin' on the bus. We'll show them to ye as soon as we get to Longford.'

She wouldn't budge. She kept her hand out. Luckily someone called her away.

With that we got on the bus and hid down the back beside Harry Hennessy. Flintstone didn't show up. I thought that very odd.

Harry had plenty of sandwiches with him, sardines in tomato sauce. Only some of the lads didn't like sardines, and the others didn't like tomato sauce. So we handed them back to Harry. He had them all eaten before we got clear of Dublin on the road to Longford.

We dodged Mrs O'Leary when we got to Longford, and went up the town for a while with Harry. He brought us into a pub and bought us Coca-Cola.

'What time's the match over at?' he asked.

'Half-five.'

'Tell the coach-driver to pick me up here afterwards. I'll be good and ready for a quarter to six.'

We checked the name of the pub and went back to the pitch.

Mrs O'Leary was waiting for us. She was boiling with rage.

Seems she had gone into Dunnes Stores the previous day to buy a ton of black and white pudding, twenty kilos of sausages, ten large sliced pans, four packets of tea and loads of other groceries for her clan. She had walked

into Flintstone McKay while in the store. He was wearing the Dunnes Stores' shop gear.

'What're you doin' here?' she asked him.

'Jus' doin' a message.'

'Doin' a message! Well, if you're only doin' a message why are you wearin' that jumper with Dunnes Stores written all over it?'

Flintstone wasn't going to answer. Before you could blink an eye, he was gone. Vanished in the crowd and ran out the back to hide.

Mrs O'Leary called a supervisor over.

'What's that Flintstone McKay doin' here?' she bellowed at him.

'He's helpin' pack the shelves.'

'Packin' shelves? What age do you have to be to work here?'

'Sixteen.'

Mrs O'Leary nearly died. The eyes rolled in her head, her face turned puce and she went bananas.

'Sixteen?'

All of sudden, she knew for certain Flintstone was over age. Coming so quickly on Chippy being found out it probably meant that the rest of us were over age as well.

'Sixteen!' she roared again, hit by the full horror of what she thought was Flintstone's true age.

But it wasn't quite that bad. Flintstone was only fourteen. Like with the Gaelic team, he had lied and said he was sixteen, so as to get the job with Dunnes Stores. And what was wrong with that? Most of us told lies. Even Mrs O'Leary was a liar. It was a fact of life.

She must have had a dreadful night, that

night. Wanting to win at all costs. And hoping against hope that her star players weren't over age too.

Anyway, now that the truth was out she wouldn't let us on to the pitch until we produced our birth-certs. She cornered us in the dressing-room and we had no choice but to hand them over.

We were out in the cold.

She wouldn't let us play.

Eddie Marsden hated us. You could see by the way he stared that he really hated us.

'You could have ruined me! One step out on the pitch an' I was ruined,' were the last words we heard Mrs O'Leary screech before we bolted from the dressing-room.

We didn't hang around the ground either. We didn't say where we were going. We belted off down the road as fast as we could, our football bags bouncing up and down on our shoulders.

We went back to the pub to Harry Hennessy. He didn't want to know. Didn't care.

'How're we goin' to get home, Harry?'

'What d'ye mean?'

'They won't pick us up in the bus. We've no way of gettin' home.'

'We'll get the train home when the pub closes.'

'There'll be no trains when the pubs close.'

'Well, I'm not movin' till the pub closes.'

'Maybe there'll be a goods train,' sulked someone.

'Maybe,' said Harry Hennessy, kind of offhand. 'Maybe. If not we'll walk out the road an' sleep in a hayshed.'

Sleep in a hayshed? It was that bad. And after coming so close to playing in Croke Park. Coming so close to ruining Mrs O'Leary.

We felt brutal. We sat there and watched Harry Hennessy drink pints for a while. Then we went out and had a look around Longford. We felt like going back to where the match was being played and letting the air out of the coach tyres. But we hadn't the heart. We were totally crushed.

We had started out to get the better of Mrs O'Leary, make a show of her.

But it was the other way around now.

She had a bus to go home in – a bed to sleep in. She didn't have to sleep in a hayshed; we did.

We hid in the toilet most of the way home. Only we weren't all in the one toilet; we split up.

Going up the estate some lad shouted over to me, 'Ye didn't do very well in the match in Longford, did ye?'

'Wha' d'ye mean?'

'Gettin' beaten by four goals an' six points.'

Four goals and six points! No wonder the other team was called the Longford Slashers.

That meant Eddie Marsden and company were out of the competition. No Croke Park, no medals, no nothing.

So what?

I didn't care about Mrs O'Leary any more, either. All I wanted to do was climb into bed and go to sleep.

Mrs O'Leary?

I just didn't give a damn about her.

12 Mad Victor Escapes

We tried our best to keep away from Mrs O'Leary, Eddie Marsden and Margo for a while. We knew they'd have it in for us for what happened in Longford. But after a few weeks Mr Glynn and Harry Hennessy wanted us down in the People's Park for pre-season training.

We tried every trick in the book not to go near the Park. In the end, we agreed to go, but only when Eddie Marsden and Margo weren't using the pitch. We were that afraid to go anywhere near it if there was a chance of them being around.

It took a while before we got rid of our fear. But the expected trouble never came about.

The only good thing about Eddie Marsden and Margo still using our pitch was that the grass was cut all the time. Usually during the summer it turned into a meadow, and the only thing it was good for was crawling on your belly, letting on you were a Jap, or to hide in if you wanted to call names at the oul' ones passing by on the road.

Much to our rage, Mrs O'Leary was going from strength to strength on the Council. Chippy said it wasn't because she was brainier than the others, or that the others were thicker than her. It was because she shouted louder than them. She was never done shouting. 'If they shout, you shout louder,' was her motto.

You hadn't got to buy a newspaper to hear what she had to say at the Council meetings. All you had to do was stand inside the main door, and it would all float down the stairs, straight into your ear. She never shut up. No wonder her husband was a nervous wreck. And never mind battered husbands. What about battered Councillors?

Then suddenly Mrs O'Leary seemed to lose interest in the issues that had got her elected. She lost all interest in us, sport, playing fields for kids. Suddenly, she was more interested in turning perfectly good streets into one-way streets, and vice-versa. She got so mixed up that she wanted to build houses where there was nothing, and knock down houses where there were plenty. She was out to make a proper mess of the town. But we didn't mind, once she left us and our football pitch alone.

We still had it in for her over Mad Victor, though.

But after a month that all passed away too.

You see, Mad Victor and his brother escaped from the Home they were being kept in.

It happened one night. They got out of a window and ran to the nearby railway line,

where they climbed into one of the wagons on a goods train that had pulled into a siding to let another train go by. The goods train was pointed in the direction of Dublin. They thought if they got that far they'd be well able to make it on their own to Bray and home.

Only the goods train didn't stop in Dublin. It sped through every station on the line and didn't halt until it got to Arklow. The boys got off, thinking they were in a railway station. They went into an office and asked the man behind the desk for two half fares to Bray.

'What… what do you think this is?'

'A railway station.'

'This isn't a railway station.'

'Wha's it then?'

'It's a factory.'

And it was. The NET factory in Arklow. Nitrogen Eireann. Makes fertilisers.

The man held Mad Victor and his brother in the office and phoned the gardai.

The two lads got back to Bray a few hours later. Only it wasn't by train, it was in a squad-car. Their uncles were delighted to see them;

they vowed Victor and Henry would never be put in a Home again. And they weren't. Any time a stranger came near the house they'd run and hide.

They spent a lot of time hiding. All that was left of the summer and most of the winter. After that the social workers gave up on them and things got back to normal.

We were all delighted for Mad Victor. What was even better, we had him back on our football team. The team would never have been the same without him – we would have lost our true identity.

Now we were whole again.

We were Riverside. There was no one in Bray or Dublin who didn't know us. What was more, soon as our soccer season started, Eddie Marsden and Margo took their goal-posts down and went off to the spanking resodded pitch Mrs O'Leary had pushed through from the Council.

We were delighted to see Eddie Marsden, Margo and their goal-posts go. We were over the moon.

What was more, we never got any interference from them, or Mrs O'Leary, again.

We felt real good about that. We felt we had fought a war, and won. It was good to be in a war. And it was even better to win. The pitch was ours again. We had fought the war, *and won*.

13 Two Broken Hearts

Da was worried about Fiona and Kathleen, my two sisters. Lots of fellows were beginning to hang around the front gate at night, wanting to take them out.

Ever since Heather McFadden had come around to the house and done something for their faces, the fellows had become very keen on my sisters.

Da felt as mad as hell over it. He became real cross, always giving out. He just couldn't stand the sight of fellows standing outside the gate. Sometimes he'd go out and run them off, but they'd be back half an hour later.

One night, when he went outside to run the fellows away from the gate, he came roaring back into the house.

'The car's gone!'

'What d'ye mean?'

'It isn't there any more! Someone's after robbin' it!'

'Not there?' said Ma.

'No, it's gone!'

As for me, I was glad. I was fed up shoving it up and down the road, trying to get it started. I'd been shoving it that much I was getting huge muscles.

But I felt sorry for Ma.

Only a few days ago she'd put a geranium in the back window of the car, so it would get the sun. I think that was why she was so upset. It wasn't over the car; it was because of the geranium.

'I couldn't see them gettin' very far, Da. The car only goes a little bit, then conks out. It's probably down the road somewhere.'

Ma and Da went down the road, looking for the car. They didn't have far to look. The front was bent around a steel lamp-post, with the windscreen smashed on the ground.

Da took it very badly. The car was no good any more, not even for sitting in and reading the paper. It was only fit for the scrap-yard. And that's where it ended up, though it took a while to get it towed away. Da hadn't got the

money to pay to get it moved. So we had to leave it around the lamp-post until he got someone to do it on the cheap.

The gardai started coming to the house, giving out about it.

'When are you going to move the car?'

'Soon as I get things fixed up.'

'You said the same last week.'

'It takes time. I'll have it out of there next Tuesday.'

The milkman took it on tow and brought it to the scrap-yard. He got £40, which he kept for towing the car away.

We got nothing, except Ma got her geranium back. It's on the kitchen window and doing real well.

In the end I was glad the car was gone. Apart from not having to shove it any more Da became real serious after losing it and didn't laugh as much. He wasn't totally cured of his donkey laugh. But as he didn't laugh as much as before it was almost as good as a cure.

So it was just as well someone stole the car and crashed it into a pole.

Whoever it was did us a favour. We couldn't have thanked him enough.

Soon after, it was announced on the telly that the winner of the book competition I'd hoped to win would be announced on the 30th of September in Jury's Hotel, Ballsbridge. I went along to hear the result.

The place was full of people. The baldy lad from the telly was there.

For a second, I thought I saw Chippy. But

when I looked again he wasn't to be seen. Either way, it couldn't have been Chippy. There was no way Chippy would turn up in a place like that. Not with all those posh people around.

After a while, the baldy lad made a speech. Then he introduced one of the judges who had made the choice as to the best book.

'How refreshing,' he said, 'to read a story about real boys. One that is true to life. I get so tired of all these half-baked problem stories that abound.'

Then he announced, 'The winner is *Soccer King* by John O'Brien.'

Next thing, Chippy stepped forward out of the crowd to accept the prize.

As soon as I heard Chippy's name being mentioned I nearly died on the spot. Not only had I not won, but now I'd never be able to write my great football story. Ever. It was already written. By Chippy!

I could feel tears come into my eyes. I couldn't take any more. I bolted through the door, and didn't stop until I got to the Dart station at Lansdowne Road.

All I could think of was Chippy robbing all my ideas for *Soccer King*. Chippy won with the story I would have written. Some pal!

By now, the tears weren't just in my eyes. They were all down my face, trickling on to my good white shirt and school tie. I vowed I'd never talk to Chippy again.

Just then, I remembered seeing that film, *Gone with the Wind.* I remembered seeing the end with the one crying and saying, 'Tomorrow is another day'.

I sat on the bench further up the platform and waited for the train ... waited for tomorrow to come.

Nothing surer, I'd get my own back on Chippy.

Because after all, I suddenly realised:

Tomorrow is another day.

Peter Regan

Riverside: The Street League

Mrs O'Leary has a GREAT IDEA. Start a street-league! To keep all the tea-leaves around the place out of trouble. And get a little publicity – which might come in handy in view of impending Council elections.

Riverside to a man – or a U-14 – rise to the challenge. Which team will bring home the Brenda O'Leary Perpetual Cup?

But, of course, football is not the only thing on their minds. Chippy has his gran to worry about. Jimmy has to sort out his da, write a book, and dream about the beautiful Heather McFadden. Mad Victor has his own ideas; especially where Mrs O'Leary is concerned ...

Illustrated by Terry Myler • £2.95

PETER REGAN, born in north Roscommon, now lives in Bray, where he runs a small fuel and seed business. He writes about soccer from personal experience; he once managed a schoolboy team, and as 'Chick' Regan masterminded the Avon Glens and Brighton Celtic. Today he is a spectator, following the fortunes of Liverpool and Glasgow Celtic.

He has written three soccer books: *Urban Heroes, Teen Glory* and *Young Champions,* which have been very successful here and have also been translated into several European languages. He has also written two fantasy books: *Touchstone* and *Revenge of the Wizards.*

Riverside: The Croke Park Conspiracy is the second in the 'Riverside' series. First was *Riverside: The Street-League,* and he has already written a third.